A WINTER'S JOURNEY

A WINTER'S JOURNEY

PHIL JORDAN

Copyright © 2025 Phil Jordan.

All rights reserved. No part of this book may be used or reproduced by any means, graphic, electronic, or mechanical, including photocopying, recording, taping or by any information storage retrieval system without the written permission of the author except in the case of brief quotations embodied in critical articles and reviews.

This is a work of fiction. All of the characters, names, incidents, organizations, and dialogue in this novel are either the products of the author's imagination or are used fictitiously.

Archway Publishing books may be ordered through booksellers or by contacting:

Archway Publishing
1663 Liberty Drive
Bloomington, IN 47403
www.archwaypublishing.com
844-669-3957

Because of the dynamic nature of the Internet, any web addresses or links contained in this book may have changed since publication and may no longer be valid. The views expressed in this work are solely those of the author and do not necessarily reflect the views of the publisher, and the publisher hereby disclaims any responsibility for them.

Any people depicted in stock imagery provided by Getty Images are models, and such images are being used for illustrative purposes only. Certain stock imagery © Getty Images.

ISBN: 978-1-6657-7180-1 (sc)
ISBN: 978-1-6657-7182-5 (hc)
ISBN: 978-1-6657-7181-8 (e)

Library of Congress Control Number: 2025900667

Print information available on the last page.

Archway Publishing rev. date: 2/12/2025

CHAPTER 1

It was the last day of school before Christmas vacation. Vida Rose skipped home clinging to her most prized possession, her Autograph Book. She climbed the front steps, opened one side of the double doors, entering the foyer. As the door slammed behind her the twist bell in the door echoed a faint ring. She removed her knit hat and scarf, put her mittens in her pocket and took off her winter Mackinaw. She hung her winter coat on the hall tree in the foyer, unbuckled her galoshes and placed them in the tray to catch the drippings of the melting snow.

The clanging of the piano by the stairway caught her attention, reminding her that Mrs. Benson was having her weekly piano lesson. Vida Rose's mother, Mary Kathleen, had been giving piano lessons to supplement her income since her husband John had enlisted and was fighting the war in Europe. Her husband John, Vida Rose's father, had been missing in action and presumed dead since the D-Day invasion on June 6, 1944. Three months after the invasion Mary Kathleen had received a letter from John, postmarked June 5th. In the letter, he talked of his fears but more so of his love for Mary Kathleen, Vida Rose, and her brother John Jr., nicknamed Junior. The letter carried a theme of intuitive doom. It never mentioned the pending invasion, showing John's loyalty to his country and his patriotic devotion to the military, although he obviously knew of the invasion through his orders, but obviously maintained military secrecy.

Miss Benson, or 'Old Lady Benson' as most of the kids called her, had taken lessons for several years, but hadn't progressed to play anything recognizable. Miss Benson worked in the ice cream parlor in the center of town. The scowl on her face was permanent and seemed to create a fear of saying or doing the wrong thing in her presence, frightful to the kids who sought sweetness in the ice cream shoppe.

Vida Rose ascended the stairs as rapidly as possible, hoping to get to her room without any formalities. Halfway up the stairs, her mother, Mary Kathleen said, "We mustn't be rude, Vida Rose, say hello to Miss Benson."

"Hello Miss Benson," Vida Rose said in the faint and timid voice of a nine-year-old schoolgirl.

Miss Benson nodded without saying a word, her squinty eyes piercing through her thick glasses. Miss Benson's scowl was uninterrupted. She never changed. Her hair was braided and wrapped around her head several times, and she always wore the same dark blue-white polka dot taffeta dress. Her piercing glance sent chills into Vida Rose, as she turned and hastened more quickly to the top of the stairs.

"Any word from father?" Vida Rose inquired.

"Nothing in today's mail, maybe tomorrow" Mary Kathleen responded dejectedly, giving hope daily to her fears as well as those of her children. Mary Kathleen and Miss Benson sat in silence for a few moments in what appeared to be prayerful reflection, not knowing what to say to one another. The silence resolved the awkwardness of the moments and the piano lesson proceeded.

Vida ran to her room, still clutching the Autographed Book that never strayed too far from her reach.

She sat on the edge of the bed and opened the book. The first page contained the autograph for which the page was reserved. Hoddie Davies was an upperclassman two years older, who had caught the fancy of Vida Rose the previous summer. His dark brown hair, parted in the middle, embraced his hazel eyes. He was a tall, gangly sort of kid who rapidly became the object of Vida Rose's affection. Of course, it was a very carefully guarded secret, held only in the heart of Vida Rose. She was in love at last, finally realizing she would not be an old maid at nine years old.

She carefully opened the autograph book as the pages were detaching from its binding from so many endearing openings. She cast her eyes upon the inscription reading each word carefully:

"Roses are red, violets are blue,

Puppies are cute,

But not as cute as you."

Hoddie Davies (December 1944)

She pressed the autographed book with both hands against her heart, staring into the future that lay ahead in her dreams. After several moments of childhood fantasy of her new-found love, she closed the book, hid it under her pillow, laid on her side and drifted off to sleep.

It was in her first moments of slumber that she found herself wading through knee-deep snow. It was difficult walking, the cold chilled her to the bone. Everything was made stark white by the snowfall that covered the surroundings. She had no idea where she was, there were no trees or anything to note, except a huge, beautiful castle that shimmered on the horizon. The castle resembled a palace made of ice, with spires reaching to the sky. The snow continued to fall. There was no sun, only the gray skies of winter.

A wrought iron fence and massive gate surrounded the castle giving way to its entrance. The fence and the gate had a mother-of-pearl appearance to it as if it were alabaster frosted by the winter weather. On one side of the gate stood a beautiful white carriage trimmed in gold and precious jewels. A stately pure white horse was harnessed to the carriage, the harness bedecked with jewels and a large white plume rising above the horse's head. On the other side of the gate was a shiny black carriage with silver trimmings, and a large black horse harnessed to it, with silver buttons outlining the harness, and a black plume waving above the horse's head.

Vida Rose shivered in the cold but continued to walk forward hoping to find warmth in the palatial Castle. As she approached the castle gate, a beautiful woman descended the steps and walked toward her holding a single stem red rose in her hand. It seemed odd that it was snowing outside the castle gate, yet the sun was shining inside the gate. As the lady approached, Vida Rose could see a beauty in her like in no other. The woman had silky smooth skin that seemed bronze in color. Her hair was dark, almost black. It was braided and hung in loops below each ear. Her eyes were chocolate brown filled with love and compassion. They seemed to open the doors to one's soul. She donned a white sable fur band about her head, nestled with Holly. She wore a long deep red velvet robe, cloaked with a white sable stole about her shoulders. The beautiful lady opened the gate and stood in the opening.

"So, you are Vida Rose!" Her voice was so soft and gentle, giving warmth to Vida as she stood before the woman.

She handed the rose to Vida, "This is a reminder of the beauty of creation. As long as you hold onto it you will have a warmth like no other. It will be a constant reminder of hope in your journey." Her hand touched Vida's forehead and a warmth immediately went throughout her body. Her hand reminded Vida of her mother's hand caressing her brow in moments of distress, or fear.

"All journeys begin with a decision as to their destination and how to get there," the lady began. "Your first decision in your journey is to decide whether you want to go in the white coach or in the black coach. A simple decision, but one of great consequence."

Without hesitation Vida Rose responded, "I choose the white carriage, it seems fitting for a princess, and my Papa always called me, 'Princess', so I choose the white carriage."

"Remember most of the decisions on your journey will be your decisions, choose wisely, rely on others, and know you are loved," the lady offered her wisdom as she helped Vida Rose into the majestic white carriage.

"Let the journey begin," the lady commanded in a firm but gentle voice. The horse began a gentle stride, and the carriage began to glide across the snow as if never touching the ground.

She had not gone far in her journey when she heard her mother's voice call her name. She looked around and could not see her mother. A second time her mother's voice called, "Vida………. Vida

Rose." She still could not locate her mother. On the third cry she opened her eyes from her slumber, as her mother's hand was gently touching her forehead.

"You were in a deep sleep; do you feel okay?" Mary Kathleen inquired. "You feel a bit feverish, perhaps you should stay in bed, and I will bring you some broth. Put on your nightgown, a good night's rest can't hurt a bit. We have several days of celebrating Christmas, and you need your rest."

"Mother, I just had the most unusual and beautiful dream," she began. "I dreamt I was walking through deep snow. The only thing visible was a beautiful castle. It was like it was made of ice but yet the sun was shining, and it didn't melt. There were two carriages parked on the street by its gates. One was a beautiful white ornate carriage drawn by a huge white horse, the other a black carriage drawn by a big black horse. A beautiful woman dressed in a red velvet robe and white fur cape came to the gate. She gave me a long-stemmed red rose, told me beautiful things and said I had to choose whether to begin my journey in the white carriage or the black carriage. She was so beautiful............... I was in the carriage and just as it began to move, I heard you call to me three times and suddenly I awakened. I so wanted to see where the carriage would take me."

"Perhaps your dream will continue when you go back to sleep. In the meantime, you must have some chicken broth and tea to break that fever." Mary Kathleen went downstairs to the kitchen to prepare the broth and hot tea, hoping to ward off any illness that might ruin the Christmas holiday.

The holidays would be difficult enough without John, but she had the love of their children to see her through these troubled times. Her fearful thoughts turned to John's last embrace, offering her the comfort and consolation that he would always be with her. She could hear his voice echo through the past several months, "I love you to the moon and back, a million miles could never separate our love." A tear descended her cheek as the warmth of his words once again embraced her with a renewed strength of spirit and hope.

CHAPTER 2

Mary Kathleen removed the mason jar containing the chicken stock from the icebox. Whenever she cooked chicken, she held the stock in reserve, for just such needs, soups, culinary delights, and medicinal potions.

As she stirred the stock into some boiling water, John Junior sat at the kitchen table eating some shepherd's pie. Mary Kathleen had prepared the shepherd's pie that afternoon. It was John Junior's favorite, except for the carrots, which he readily fed to Bowser. Bowser the family dog lay playing under the table, waiting for a morsel of food to drop. Mary Kathleen caught John's escapade out of the corner of her eye. "I'm sure Bowser appreciates those carrots and they probably will improve his eyesight, but they also will improve the eyesight of a growing boy," Mary Kathleen chastised. "Don't forget mothers have eyes in the back of their heads."

"I'm taking some broth and hot tea up to Vida Rose, she's a bit under the weather and we need her well for the holiday. I'll be right back. We need to have a talk." Mary Kathleen said in a determined voice.

"What about?" Junior inquired.

"About Naomi!" Mary Kathleen responded as she left the kitchen with a tray of broth and tea in her hands.

"That 'old 'Injun' woman' is crazy," Junior yelled as Mary Kathleen climbed the stairs.

"We'll talk soon young man," his mother's voice became more sternly disciplined.

As Mary Kathleen opened the bedroom door Vida Rose slid the autographed book under her pillow. She had read the inscription so many times it was ingrained into her mind so that all she had to do was close her eyes and she could see the inscription and the young man who had written it. Seeing it in the well-worn autograph book simply validated her dreams.

"How are you feeling, my dear? You look a bit peaked," Mary Kathleen said with concern in her voice and the intuitive fears of a mother.

"My throat's a little sore, but I'm sure the broth and hot tea will make it better." Vida said.

As Mary Kathleen laid the palm of her hand across her daughter's forehead, she realized the fever had worsened. "I think I'll put a call in to Dr. Tinker and see if he can stop by, if not tonight, in the morning. We don't need a sore throat to go into strep throat as part of our Christmas celebration."

Vida Rose had already drifted back to sleep. Mary Kathleen roused her to drink some of the broth and tea. It was obvious that her throat was sore. She drank half a cup of broth and a couple swallows of tea but refused anymore. She lay her head back on the pillow and was asleep in a matter of moments. Mary Kathleen thought it best to let her sleep.

Mary Kathleen went to the phone in the hallway by the stairs and cranked two longs and a short on the crank telephone. She had to stand on her tip toes to talk into the mouthpiece. As she held the receiver to her ear, she could hear the voice of her neighbor Naomi talking on the ten party line. Naomi had a recognizably distinct voice from her Native American heritage. Naomi's husband was in the military as well and was serving his country as a Navajo Code Talker. The Army commissioned many of the men of his culture to serve the country with their native tongue so that the Japanese could not identify secret communications. Naomi was very proud of him for serving his country and bringing pride to his people.

"I'm sorry, Naomi, but I have to get through to Dr. Tinker, I have a sick girl on my hands."

"I'll get off immediately so you can use the phone. If there's anything I can do please let me know." Naomi said in her usual compassionate way.

"I will, and thank you for clearing the phone, May God Bless," Mary Kathleen responded.

Once again Mary Kathleen cranked two longs and a short. The phone rang several times before Mary Kathleen heard the voice of Mrs. Tinker answer the phone, "Dr. Tinker's office."

"Hello Mrs. Tinker, this is Mary Kathleen McDuffie, is Dr. Tinker available?"

"Oh no, he is over to Mary Teresa Finley's delivering her seventh child. Seven children!!! Wouldn't you think they would know where they come from by now. But that seems to be a Catholic thing. Now my husband's grandmother was Catholic, but she only had three children, two of them went off to college and her son was a drunkard who did nothing with his life," Mrs. Tinker carried on, talking incessantly.

Mary Kathleen interrupted, "Perhaps you could have Dr. Tinker come by in the morning as my Vida Rose is down with a sore throat and it seems to be worsening."

"Okay, I will leave a note on the table for the doctor, and he will come over in the morning." Mrs. Tinker seemed abrupt as Mary Kathleen interrupted her diatribe of family history and perpetual gossip.

As she hung up the phone Mary Kathleen said to herself, "Mary, Joseph, and Jesus, the woman could talk an ear off an iron pig. Who cares about the drunkards in her family. She obviously forgot I'm a confessed Catholic in good standing."

As he swung open the kitchen door, Junior stood at the back door in his wool hat with ear flaps, a scarf around his neck and his winter coat. The dog wagging his tail beside him was anxious to go out.

"I'm going to take Bowser for a walk" he chimed.

"We must chat about Naomi," Mary Kathleen said as she pulled out the chair from the kitchen table to sit down. "Take off your hat and coat and come sit at the table."

Hesitantly, Junior took off his hat, gloves, and coat, stuffing the hat and gloves in the sleeve of his coat and hanging it on the corner post of the back of the chair. He began talking as he slid onto the chair seat.

"She's a mean old woman. I don't like the way her eyes stare at me when she sees me. Sometimes I can't understand what she says and it makes no sense. She's always talking about the great father and how he will bring my father home. It's been almost 7 months and there's no sign of father, and I'm tired of her gibberish."

"Young man, she is a proud Native American of Navajo heritage. Her husband is serving our country well as a Navajo Code Talker so that the enemy will not know what our plans are in the war. It may be her husband's work that will help us to find your father. Just because she's different doesn't mean she can't be loved. The Great Father that she speaks of is the same God of our understanding, as she knows and understands him. Her name "Naomi" is a biblical name meaning 'wise 'or wise woman. I trust it would be in your best interest to trust a wise woman. You mustn't allow your soul to become bitter and prejudice against any person that our loving father in heaven has created. It is a shameful thing to do so. Tonight when we go to bed I will deal with you at your bedside and we shall say the rosary together, asking God's forgiveness for your thoughtless thinking, continued prayers for your father and Naomi's husband, and especially for your sister, Vida Rose for her recovery."

John Junior was already feeling remorse for his thoughts and actions against Naomi. He knew how long and extensive the prayers would be before he could jump into a warm bed on a winters evening. His punishment was already evident. He hoped that his mother wouldn't find out that he was the one that would run along Naomi's picket fence with a stick against the pickets making a loud clicking sound. He noticed that such activity had already scratched the whitewashed fence. He not only felt fear but began to feel guilt which was part of his punishment. It was also the sign of a good conscience.

Meanwhile, Vida Rose had hastily gone back into a deep sleep. She found herself in the white carriage with the red rose in her hand. The scent of the raspberry red rose brought the rose to her nose and lips. As she touched the rose to her lips, suddenly the Snow Queen was riding in the seat across from her.

"You want to talk?" the Snow Queen's gentle voice resounded in its' familiarity. "Your lips bring the beauty of your soul to creation. What comes across your lips let the world know who you are. As your lips have touched the rose, they beckoned me to come and be with you. Do you wish to ask something?"

The normally inquisitive and chatty Vida Rose was in awestruck and awkward silence.

"I know that you yearn to be with your father, and soon you shall be, but patience is a virtue and that cannot happen until it is meant for that to happen. Know that he loves you and wants to be with you and will be soon. That is a promise I can make to you." The beautiful lady vanished as quickly as she had appeared. A white rose remained on the red velvet seat where the woman sat. Vida Rose knew instinctively a white rose meant friendship which even more strengthened the trust in the Snow Queen. She knew her journey would lead her to her father. The carriage seemed airborne. Vida Rose could see beautiful mountains and valleys with small towns in each Valley. She noticed the white church steeples in each town and thought of her own faith and her First Communion. She went by the first school she attended, a little white one-room schoolhouse where everyone had fun. The teacher Miss Ida was a strict teacher. She too had squinty eyes and reminded Vida Rose of Miss Benson. On the stoop of the boy's entrance sat Tommy O'Malley. She remembered the day Tommy got in trouble for dipping the end of her pigtail in his inkwell as he sat behind her. Suddenly she thought, how could that be Tommy waving from the stoop when he had drowned in the river during the spring thaw last year. But it was Tommy. He had the same dimples, the impish smile, and the gleam in his eye that portrayed his mischievousness. She was so glad to see him, but the horse sped up and it was a passing reunion.

The horse soon found its way to the front of a hospital. It was a military hospital. As she saw all the people in uniform, it brought her back to the memories of her father. What a striking man he was in uniform. If only she could see him and know that he was well.

She touched the rose to her lips and once again the beautiful lady appeared. "You want to ask if your father is in this hospital," the lady uttered. Just as she said that Vida Rose found herself standing at the foot of the bed in which her father was sleeping. In the bed next to his was a dark-skinned man whose eyes narrowed at the corners. She knew he wasn't Oriental, but she knew he was of some other race. The old man's face seemed wrinkled and weathered with years of fighting life's battles.

"Papa, it's me Vida Rose. Oh, father please wake up," she could feel the warmth of her tears running down her cheeks. Her father opened his eyes, turned his head, stared into the large room and went back to sleep. Vida Rose touched the rose to her lips and found herself back in the carriage seated in front of the Snow Queen.

"Why did he not know that I was there?

"It was a spiritual visit, your love reconnected your spirits, he knew you were there and you know that you were with him, it's love and the love your soul yearns for in its longing."

Just as Vida Rose was about to ask the lady if her father was alive or dead, she was awakened by her mother's voice.

"I saw Papa, he was in an Army hospital, but I couldn't wake him up. There was an old man in the bed next to his and I remember, the old man, he smiled and winked at me. I felt everything was going to be okay."

Mary Kathleen leaned over and put her cheek next to her daughter's. She whispered in her ear. "You've had a dream, and everything will be okay. I am sure your father is thinking of you and you're thinking of your father. Wherever he is, his love is with us. We must trust that and continue to pray for him."

"How could it be a dream when it was so real. I even saw my old school chum, Tommy O'Malley, sitting on the stoop of the school and he was waving to me. I know it was him but how could it be, he died?"

Mary Kathleen comforted her daughter, "My Grandmother told me that the Irish people believe that when we dream of the dead they actually come to visit us and we create a dream around it so it's more believable." As she finished saying that she realized that she was telling her daughter for the first time that her father may be dead. It was done unconsciously and accidentally but perhaps it needed to be done after all these months of her husband John missing in action and presumed dead. It also told Mary Kathleen that she was beginning to accept that dire fact as well. Vida Rose's dream of her father and the unfortunate loss of her school chum, Tommy O'Malley, brought Mary Kathleen some superstitious worry.

Once again, Vita Rose drifted off to sleep and continued her journey. She touched the rose once again to her lips. The Snow Queen once again sat in her presence. "Is it possible that I may go once again to where my father was in the hospital? I just need to see him one more time before I make any more decisions." She had scarcely finished her sentence and found herself standing at the foot of her father's bed. Her father and the older man with the dark wrinkled skin were engaged in a conversation. Her father seemed uncertain as to everything he said. The old man asked him how he had gotten to the hospital. He said "I couldn't remember anything they diagnosed it as shell-shocked from the D-Day invasion into Normandy. My dog tags were missing, and I had no other identification on me. Supposedly, the cleanup detail found me in a German bunker overlooking Omaha Beach. It appeared I had cleared the bunker of the enemy, but they think a grenade may have gone off and caused a severe concussion, or shell-shock, which caused the amnesia as to who I am or where I belong. They said apparently the Germans thought I was dead, so they left my body with their dead comrades. The only thing I had on me was this picture. It was wrapped and taped in cellophane, they figured it must be a picture of my wife and two children."

He handed the sepiatone brown picture still wrapped in cellophane to his newfound friend. The older man squinted for several moments. He said, "the little girl in this picture looks just like the little girl next door to where I live back home. Her name is Vida Rose."

"That's right Papa, I am Vida Rose and I am here with you, please hear me!" The two men continued to talk paying no attention to Vida's anxious pleas.

"Her mother was named Mary Kathleen, and her brother, I think, was named John Jr.. The little girl had vivid red curls, thousands of freckles and crystal blue eyes that could sink a battleship with compassion. The father enlisted against the mother's wishes about a year before I was called to duty. I didn't see much of them because I was called to duty shortly after moving into the house next to them. The little girl had helped my wife with the rose garden along our front picket fence. She was a sweetheart." He handed the picture back to Vida Rose's father. John stared at the picture for 15 or 20 minutes, and soon tears were streaming down his face. "The name of the street you lived on wasn't by any chance, Humiston Street was it?"

"Well yes, yes it was, how did you know that?" The old man replied.

"Because I lived at 16, Humiston St. and the house next door was 14 Humiston, and it had a picket fence and rose garden at the front gate," John said choking back tears. The old man grabbed the hand-bell that was on his nightstand and rang for the attending nurse. John looked away to hide his tears and envisioned sitting with his mother as a child in church as they sang the words, "I once was lost but now I'm found." He sobbed uncontrollably.

The joy that filled Vida Rose's heart was overwhelming, now she could continue her journey. She kissed her father's tear-soaked cheek as he continued to stare at the picture and replenish his mind with a lifetime of wonderful memories. Vida Rose could continue her journey with the knowledge that her father had not died in that awful war. Once again, she found herself in the white carriage.

Vida Rose's fever had not broken, if anything it had worsened. The glands in her throat had swollen and her breathing had become raspy. Mary

Kathleen kissed her on the forehead, turned out the light and left her with the thought that a good night's sleep would give her rest and ward off the on-setting illness.

CHAPTER 3

The grandfather clock in the foyer was striking 8 AM. Mary Kathleen was putting up her hair, placing the last tortoiseshell comb in the up sweep of her hair, when she heard the grinding of the front doorbell. She could see through the frosted etched glass of the oval windows the outline of a man. A short man, rather plump, with the signature bowler hat that Dr. Tinker always wore. She hastened to the door opening it to the Jolly red-faced, sparse red-haired man with a cropped beard, red with gray highlights. His round wire spectacles rested on his plump red cheeks. He removed his hat as she opened the door.

"Good morning, Mary Kathleen," Dr. Tinker stated in a professional yet neighborly way as he walked past Mary Kathleen into the foyer.

"Thank the good Lord you are here, please come in," Mary Kathleen in a concerned and hopeful voice.

He hung his hat on the hall tree, adjusted his collar, picked up his leather doctors' bag and began walking towards the stairs, a journey he had obviously taken several times before.

"So how is our girl this morning?" he inquired.

"I checked her hourly through the night and she slept most of the night. The glands in her throat are swollen and her fever is very high. She complains that the back of her legs and heels hurt and she goes in and out of a very deep sleep." Mary Kathleen advised the good doctor.

"There's a lot of things going around, especially with the school kids, but let's check and see what we have going," as he began to climb the stairs.

Mary Kathleen opened the bedroom door. Dr. Tinker could see Vida Rose lying on her back, her head gently nestled in the pillow, with her bright red French curls caressing her shoulders. Hundreds of red freckles seemed more pronounced on her pale skin . The liveliness of her blue eyes was not visible under the closed lids, but he was sure they had lost their sparkle.

"My, she is feverish," he exclaimed as he touched her brow. He fumbled in his black leather bag for his stethoscope and thermometer. He was able to rouse her enough to put the thermometer under her tongue and with the help of Mary Kathleen they sat her up to listen to her heartbeat and her respirations. She was groggy and a bit incoherent perhaps from the past twelve hours of fever. He checked the glands in her throat, took the thermometer from under her tongue. He clicked his tongue three times, perhaps in concern, perhaps in fear, or perhaps that's just what doctors do.

"She's a very sick girl, her fever is 105, and it appears she has strep throat which I fear has gone into rheumatic fever. She needs penicillin immediately. Unfortunately, we are unable to get it due to the war effort. All the penicillin and such medications have to be reserved for the men and women on the front. We need to keep her hydrated, warm, and pray the good man upstairs will break her fever before it goes any further. "Mary Kathleen, Vida Rose is critically ill," the doctor stated emphatically but compassionately. As the good doctor's eyes connected with Mary Kathleen, she knew the seriousness and urgency of the situation without another word being said.

He returned the stethoscope and thermometer to the black bag and snapped it shut. As they walked down the stairs, Dr. Tinker told Mary Kathleen that he was going to place a call to a friend of his in the State Department to see if he could persuade President Roosevelt to make an exception to save Vida Rose's life. He did not mince words; it was that critical.

"I will be back this afternoon to see how things are progressing," he said assuredly as he sensed her desperation and aloneness. He put on his bowler hat, scarf, and topcoat, tipped his hat in etiquette to Mary Kathleen and closed the door behind him.

Mary Kathleen went into the 'good parlor' and sat on the elegant Victorian chair that matched the divan. The 'good parlor' was a room never used, except for special occasions or special company. Mary Kathleen sobbed openly, dabbing her linen embroidered handkerchief occasionally at each corner of her eyes. She never felt so alone. She took the photo of John off the marble top table next to her, pulling it to her bosom and sobbed uncontrollably.

"Oh, John if only you were here, things would be different, I would have the courage to go through the trials and tribulations of life. You gave me the strength to carry on, and I know if you're no longer with us in the flesh you are with us in spirit. You must know what is going on. Please come to us and give us the guidance we need."

At mid-morning Junior ran into the house with his ice skates over his left shoulder. He had been ice-skating at Smitty's Pond earlier with his school chums. As he returned home, Naomi was walking back and forth in front of the house, smudging sage and other herbs that she believed would keep the evil spirits of illness away from the house.

"Mother, mother where are you?" he ran to the kitchen as Mary Kathleen was just finishing up breakfast dishes. "That old 'injun' woman is walking back and forth in front of the house waving a bouquet of dead flowers in her hand, muttering some gibberish, and the bouquet is smoking."

"John Junior, what did I tell you about your degrading talk of Naomi.," As Mary Kathleen walked down the hallway to peer out the front window, She pulled back the lace curtain in the narrow window beside the door to see Naomi, dedicated to her faith, doing what she thought may help.

"She is doing prayers in her tongue, and the so-called burning bouquet is called smudging, it contains different herbs that she believes will keep the evil spirits away from our house and the smoke will take her prayers to God, the God of her understanding. You mustn't judge people so harshly. She is doing what she thinks will help."

"I still think she's a crazy old woman, and she gives me the creeps," Junior said.

Mary Kathleen took a deep sigh and returned to the kitchen silently chuckling to herself over the burning bouquet of dead flowers. Mary Kathleen made a fresh mug of chicken broth and tea and went upstairs to check on Vida Rose. She was still sleeping in that deep sleep, still feverish and breathing erratically. Mary Kathleen took her hand, knelt by her bed, said the 'Our Father' and several 'Hail Marys.' She placed Vida's hand against her own cheek wiping the new fallen tears from her cheek with the back of Vida's hand, caressing it with her lips and kissing the small hand. The doorbell rang and as Mary Kathleen descended the stairs, she saw Dr. Tinker standing there. She could tell by the look on his face that he was the bearer of bad news.

"Mary Kathleen, I'm sorry to say that I have gotten a telegram from the White House. President Roosevelt had seen my friend at a meeting this morning. He said he understood our plight and the gravity of the situation but, unfortunately, he could not allow one prescription to be released as it would set precedent, and he would have to honor so many other requests but couldn't. He had to follow strict protocol for the sake of the war effort. He said to be vigilant with prayer and trust in the Almighty. He and Mrs. Roosevelt would remember Vida Rose in their prayers. The telegram was sent directly from the White House, so I know he took personal interest."

Mary Kathleen simply turned in silence and ascended the stairs with the doctor following her.

"Where there's life there's hope. The President is right, we must be vigilant in prayer. We are living through times where our only hope is held in prayer." The doctor stood at the sick child's bedside, fondling his stethoscope. He listened attentively to the child's heartbeat and respiration. He stood back up, from leaning over her bed, took a deep breath and exhaled slowly. He began to talk without looking at Mary Kathleen, simply staring at the sleeping child.

"Her heartbeat has become irregular and I'm fearful that the strep infection has gone into rheumatic fever and is infecting the heart muscle. We must pray and hope for the best but be prepared for the worst."

Kathleen sat on the chair by the bed in a near faint. "Dr. Tinker, I can't lose her, I've lost John and now her. I've been faithful and good, loyal to God and his teachings, and still I'm being punished."

"Perhaps it's like the story of Job, remember all his suffering and in the end it turned out okay," the doctor said.

"Yes, but Job had to go through all of that to find his faith. I already have my faith. When will it be rewarded?" Mary Kathleen's eyes stared deep into the good doctor's eyes as he gave her a fatherly embrace.

As they approached the door, the doctor told her to keep Vida hydrated even if she had to use a rubber syringe or medicine dropper. Fluids are especially important at this time. I will be back in the morning, or sooner if you need me. If there is no change, I will see you in the morning. He tipped his hat and went out into the light snow, falling like feathers upon the earth.

CHAPTER 4

Morning dawned. There had been a light fluffy snow in the night that seemed to beckon Christmas Eve morning. Mary Kathleen had made oatmeal for Junior, fed Bowser and set Vida Rose's tray with more broth and hot tea. This morning she used her grandmother's fine China with the roses on the teapot, cup and saucer. It was such a special treat for Vida to use her great-grandmothers fine porcelain. It was Christmas Eve morning and Mary Kathleen could not begin entertaining the thought that her daughter may be dying. She was going to do everything in her motherly power to make her live.

Just as she turned to go upstairs, she heard a knock on the windowpane to the back kitchen door. She saw a short woman bent over with a gray shawl over her head and shoulders. It was Naomi. She sat the tray on the buffet and went to the door.

"Hello Naomi, what brings you out so early in the morning," Mary Catherine said as she greeted her neighbor.

"I saw your kitchen lights on and knew you must be preparing breakfast. I was fearful you wouldn't hear me at the front door so I came through the back gate." Naomi was hesitant, almost fearful that she was intruding.

"Please come in where it's warm," Mary Kathleen beckoned.

Naomi stood just inside the back door, groping for the right words. Mary Kathleen felt her uncomfortable demeanor and tried to comfort her.

"I know your little girl is desperately ill. I have not slept much this past night. I had a dream in which the Chief of our people came to me dressed in white. With him was a medicine man. The medicine man was shaking a rattle made from the rattle of a rattlesnake. I believe it to be a good sign because the medicine man was shaking evil away from us. He didn't speak for a long time, then he looked into my eyes and gave me the names of four herbs to mix together with Springwater, heat the water and herbs, and drain off the liquid, and it would help to heal the girl with hair…red, like fire. Then the medicine man turned into a white eagle and landed on the peak of your house."

"Perhaps you don't believe in dreams, much of my wisdom has come to me while my earthly body is sleeping and my spirit is still awake," Naomi said, as she looked at the floor not wanting to see how distraught Mary Kathleen was over her daughter's illness.

Naomi extended her slender bronzed hand which held an old medicine bottle with a cork. Mary Kathleen accepted the bottle although quietly apprehensive about its contents.

"Thank you so much Naomi. Your wisdom and compassion are most appreciated." Mary Kathleen embraced Naomi, not only in appreciation, but for the need of an older woman's embrace giving her some motherly affection at a most needed time.

"Give her three eyedroppers full every three hours until the rising of the full moon tonight. The full moon will light our way through this darkness."

Mary Kathleen tried to hurry the situation along as she knew the broth and tea were cooling. She felt Naomi's compassion and somehow trusted in her wisdom. She asked Naomi to join her at Vida's bedside. As they entered the room Mary Kathleen put the tray in its usual place on the nightstand next to her bed. Naomi was already whispering what appeared to be prayers in her native tongue. Naomi reached in the cloth bag flung over her shoulder and brought out what appeared to be a necklace, an intricately beaded necklace.

"This is a medicine bag I made for Vida. Can we put it around her neck, so that the bag will rest over her heart?" Naomi inquisitively asked.

Mary Kathleen felt no harm in doing so and even felt a tinge of hope and comfort come to her.

Mary Kathleen raised Vida's head as Naomi put the necklace over her head. The medicine bag lay precisely over her heart.

"I beaded the image of a turtle in the medicine bag. The turtle takes its time but always gets where it's going. Even though the recovery seems slow we must trust the medicine will get where it needs to be," Naomi said in an assuring voice.

As they laid Vida's head back on the pillow, she opened her eyes. In a faint whisper she said to her mother, "the beautiful lady promised me that before this day ends I will be with my father."

"Your father is always with you, we are all connected by love, and your father loves you very much." Mary Kathleen's eyes filled with tears as her fears seemed confirmed in Vida's own words. She continued to talk to Vida but realized as quickly as she had opened her eyes they were closed again, and she was asleep.

Once again, Vida Rose found herself traveling in the pearly white carriage, with the red velvet lining. She was so comfortable, free of any pain or earthly care. The carriage ride seemed to make life exhilarating. The carriage pulled up in front of her church, St. Luke's Chapel. Instantly, she found herself standing in the choir loft watching a group of youngsters being blessed by the Bishop in the Sacrament of Confirmation. She recognized herself and several of her friends. They appeared to be a little bit older. She turned her head to cough, looked back at the altar and saw a bride and groom at the ending of their wedding. The groom was a handsome lad in his mid-20s wearing a dark blue military uniform and a skullcap much like Hoddie Davies wore in grade school. He lifted the bride's veil and gave her a kiss. She recognized the bride to be herself, perhaps 15 years older. She felt as though she was intruding, so she made her way down the winding stairs from the choir loft near the church entrance. At the back of the church a Baptism was taking place. The man was the handsome lad that was the groom in the wedding. The mother of the newborn infant girl being baptized was once again herself, merely a few years older. Beside her at the Baptismal Font was a young lad of about six years old and a girl about three. This girl had flaming red hair. She looked exactly like Vida Rose in the pictures of her childhood. The little boy was referred to as John and the newborn infant was christened in the name of Naomi Mary Kathleen. The mother handed the baby for baptism to the Priest who resembled an older, plumper, and more red-faced Father O'Flaherty. Father O'Flaherty the priest at St. Luke's Chapel was older but still his jovial self. When the baptism had been accomplished and the baby was anointed Father O'Flaherty placed her in the arms of a very elderly Native American woman in a wheelchair.

Vida slipped out the front entrance without anyone hearing her and was in the carriage in but a moment. She picked up the rose that she had left on the seat and touched it to her lips. The Snow Queen appeared instantly.

Before the Snow Queen could ask, Vida Rose began to question her with great curiosity.

"Why did I see all those people and they didn't see me? Why did it appear to be me in all those scenes? Why did they all take place in my parish, St. Luke's Chapel? Why did the groom at the wedding and the father at the baptism wear a skullcap."

"The skullcap called a yarmulke. It is a symbol of the man's faith, the same as the cross or crucifix is a symbol of your faith. Both are symbols of humility and reverence to an abiding love for the God of your understanding. They are simply symbols of a particular religion. Religion is the shroud that faith is buried in and becomes the discipline of everyone's faith. Faithfulness is a necessary component of our spirit. Religion often becomes misunderstood, misguided, and perhaps can even become a weapon. The different beliefs among the peoples of the earth, have destroyed lives, destroyed civilizations, and confined people's progress. Be faithful don't be overly religious. Whatever a person chooses as the vehicle to arrive at their spiritual destination is part of their individual spiritual journey. Honor and respect that in yourself as well as others and you will have peace in your own heart as well as adding to peace in your world."

"The church is where you were nurtured outside the family. It holds the roots of your family's existence and your spirit. Life, as I told you before, is full of decisions. Almost all of those decisions come from our faith and a true understanding of the spirit of God that dwells in us as it mingles with our own spirit. What you have witnessed in the church are possibilities of where life's paths will lead you. All of them are based on decisions that you will make. As you have been offered the opportunity to look forward, live in the present, so you don't have to look backward with regrets. Let your conscience be your guide."

The beautiful lady had disappeared as quickly as she had appeared. Suddenly the carriage stopped at a crossroad. It was a country crossroad surrounded by beautiful fields and hills. There were no buildings, simply a country crossroad. On each corner of the crossroad, it was the same scene only in each of the four seasons. There was a sense that it symbolized the passing of time and the seasons in creation. Coming from the opposite direction and the road ahead of her she could see faintly on the horizon a horse and carriage coming toward her. As the carriage approached, her carriage remained still. The driver of the carriage had a long black cloak and a black top hat. He held the reins in a firm grip. He stared straight ahead; he did not look at Vida. A thunderous voice echoed through the valley. She knew it had come from him. "Please come with me, get in my carriage. I can take you to see your Father once again." The thought of seeing her Father was enticing. However, she remembered words from her nightly prayer "….lead us not into temptation. She listened to the foreboding feeling that had stirred within her.

"I'm happy where I am", Vida Rose said in a voice weakened by fear. But suddenly she gathered strength as she knew within herself that she had made a right decision, not only right for her, but right for the world that lay ahead. The pearly white carriage resumed its journey. Vida Rose pondered her decision. Could the other carriage take her back to all the things to which she wanted to return? Then she realized the goodness she felt with her decision. She looked back and the black carriage was already out of sight. She felt no regrets, she had made the right decision. Perhaps that is what wisdom is all about, learning from the past, and not looking back except what the past can offer the present or future.

About 1 o'clock that afternoon, Vida's condition worsened. Mary Kathleen called Dr. Tinker to come immediately. She recognized the gurgling in Vida's upper chest and throat to be what Mary Kathleen recognized as the death rattle. She had been with family on their deathbed. She knew the gurgling as to be within hours of death. Dr. Tinker came immediately.

He did his usual sequence of checking her heart and her respirations. Her heart had weakened and her lungs were filling with fluid. He turned to Mary Kathleen, "I think it best you call Father O'Flaherty, we need help beyond what I can offer. Mary Kathleen, let us remember as good Catholics we believe in miracles."

Mary Kathleen rang the rectory. Father O'Flaherty answered the phone after a few rings. The Parish secretary and housekeeper had been given the day off for Christmas Eve. "Father, the time has come, and we need you for Vida Rose," said Mary Kathleen as her voice weakened and trailed off choking back tears.

"I will be right there," Father O'Flaherty said assuredly.

CHAPTER 5

Father O'Flaherty hastily entered the front door without ringing the bell. He placed his three cornered hat with the feathery ball on top, on the sideboard in the hallway. He ascended the stairs and went into Vida's room. Several members of the family and close friends were seated or standing around the room with their focus on Vida Rose. They were silent or their lips moving in silent prayer, several reciting the Rosary. Junior sat in the corner, arms around his knees, his knees pressed against his chest and his head rested on his knees. It was obvious he did not want anyone to see his face for fear they might find tears.

Father kissed the purple and white stole and placed it around his neck. He began the liturgy for Last Rites. "In the name of the Father, and of the Son, and of the Holy Spirit." He began to pray in Latin. The scene became sacred and sorrowful. Muffled sobs could be heard among those gathered around the bed.

After a few moments of prayer, Father made the sign of the cross with his two fingers in the air and absolved Vida Rose of any earthly sin. In unison everyone said the 'Our Father', and Father O'Flaherty closed with a final blessing. Everyone crossed themselves at the final blessing, except Junior, who still had his forehead pressed against his knees. Father O'Flaherty genuflected at Vida's bedside, crossed himself once more and proceeded toward the door. As he passed Junior, he tossled his hair as if to say, I'm here if you need me.

Mary Kathleen encouraged everyone to retire to the kitchen and dining room. They sensed her need to be alone with Vida Rose. As John Junior headed for the door, she beckoned him to stay. He didn't want to for fear of showing emotions or perhaps his first physical confrontation with death. Especially the death of someone near his own age. He tried desperately to remain composed as Mary Kathleen put her arm around him. He buried his face in the bibbed apron she was wearing and sobbed uncontrollably. After a few moments, he regained his composure and Mary Kathleen asked him if he would do her a big favor.

"Would you sneak out the front door, so no one sees you, go next door, and bring Naomi back with you?" He looked up into her eyes and knew he couldn't refuse. He knew his mother's trust in Naomi negated anything bad that he had to offer.

Within seconds he was pounding on Naomi door. "Naomi, Naomi," the door opened and there stood the woman he had ridiculed, most always in her absence. "Oh, Miss Naomi, Mother needs you to come immediately, my sister is dying and Mother needs you," he said in breathless gasps. Naomi grabbed her gray shawl, made her way down the front steps of her cottage style house. She hastened as quickly as her age allowed, to be with Mary Kathleen. Junior held her arm under the left elbow each step of the way. "It's a secret, Mother does not want the others to know she has called for you," he confided in soft whispers to Naomi. As they made their way to the bedroom, Junior became aware that the secrecy was simply for the purpose of administering more of the muddy water like concoction that Naomi had made. Together Mary Kathleen and Naomi administered it to Vida Rose with a teaspoon. It seemed to remain in her throat. The gurgling worsened. All three of them, thought that she might choke but she did not.

Naomi put her arm around Mary Kathleen's waist and drew her close. Junior did the same from the her other side and found himself rubbing Naomi's outstretched arm. They remained together for several minutes. As they loosened their hold on each other, Junior gave Naomi a quick embrace, and offering of peaceful regret for his past behavior. Junior sensed a peaceful feeling about Naomi that he couldn't describe.

Mary Kathleen explained to Naomi that she wanted privacy in her visit because the others would not understand. Mary Kathleen assured Naomi that she had faith in her wisdom.

Naomi scrunched her head into her shoulders, burying her chin into her chest. As she withdrew, she smiled and winked, "so many people don't understand that there is one Great Father, he is not mine, he is not yours, he is not anyone's, he is everyone's. No matter what we believe we must be faithful. Religion is simply the discipline to be faithful." She pulled her shawl over her head so one could barely see her face, "I will go home now, call if you need me.

"May I walk you home, Naomi," Junior suddenly said, surprising even himself.

"I would be very grateful if you would, us older folk aren't so surefooted especially on winters sidewalks." Junior took her by the arm, and they began the short trek to Naomi's house.

After a few moments of silence Junior cleared his throat and said "Miss Naomi, I have said bad things about you, I am the one who has run the stick down your picket fence, and picked on you with other kids. I am so sorry; he began to cry."

"John Junior, I knew that all along, but in your bad behavior I saw your goodness, and in these bad times with Vida Rose, you got to see my goodness. Most of all, you have come to know my spirit and I have come to know yours. It is good. She opened her door and they stood in the foyer. Naomi kissed him on the forehead and said to him, "now you run home and be with your mother and sister, you're the man of the house and they need you, hurry along." He turned to go out the door, stopped, turned around and gave her an embrace that sealed their friendship. "I love you," Junior awkwardly said. Naomi scrunched her head into her shoulders once again, winked, buried her chin in her chest with modesty and said, "me too."

"As soon as the weather breaks into spring, I'm going to paint your fence," Junior said as Naomi nodded her approval. They both had found a new meaning of friendship and a new kind of love.

CHAPTER 6

The clock in the hallway was striking 8 o'clock. People had come and gone to be with Mary Kathleen at Vida's bedside, most had remained. It is such an arduous, uncomfortable and helpless feeling to sit at someone's bedside knowing that their earthly life may soon be over. Each person wants to say or do the right thing when really the only thing they can do is to share their love with those left behind. A simple "I love you", assuring the person they are not alone is probably the best advice for the occasion. Mrs. Wilkins, the town busybody, tried to get in the mournful scene. She was stopped at the door by Mary Kathleen's brother Bill. "I know exactly how Mary Kathleen feels," Mrs. Wilkins began in a shrill voice that could have cut through steel. "I lost my younger sister last year, she too went rather suddenly, it was devastating and I am just getting over it." Mrs. Wilkins sat a plate of scones she had made on the sideboard and began taking off her hat and coat. Bill immediately said to her, "Your kindness and your scones are graciously accepted, but we are trying to keep this to a private matter within the family. I hope you can understand."

"Well, Harriet Beecher, said she overheard on the party line that Vida Rose was close to death, and I thought I might be of help having been through the death of my younger sister, I know exactly what Mary Kathleen is going through," Mrs. Wilkins continued in her annoyingly high-pitched voice.

Bill was becoming more enraged. "Nice of you to come and bring the scones, but I must get back to my sister's side. I believe your younger sister was in her mid-70s and had been ill for much longer than you realized. Mary Kathleen is losing her daughter, and no one can truly know how she feels." Mrs. Wilkins continued to try to gain entrance to the house, but Bill put his arm around her shoulder and guided her to the door. "Once again, thank you for the scones, and keep everyone here in thoughtful prayer and take your curiosity and go home, I think it is there you can do the most good."

"Well,. ………………………….." Mrs. Wilkins struggled to find the words that would make Bill change his mind and allow her to be with the others. Bill ushered her out the door to the front stoop and closed the door rather abruptly behind her. He thought to himself what a wonderful thing a small community is, in the hour of need, yet, it can certainly be a detriment as everyone knows your business and wants to be involved.

The faint sounds of "Oh Come All Ye Faithful "could be heard from the street below. Mary Kathleen thought to herself how that song would never have the same meaning to her again, as the strains of "Oh Come All Ye Faithful", seemed to be calling her daughter away. She held her handkerchief to her nose and mouth to disguise a sudden sob. She remained stalwart. She returned the hanky to her apron pocket and touched the bottle with the muddy water concoction. She realized it was time to give Vida Rose another dose. She asked everyone to leave the room and return to the kitchen and dining room so that she and Junior could be alone with Vida once again. Before everyone had left the room she put her hands on Junior shoulders and whispered in his ear, "Hurry, go get Naomi," she said in an emphatic voice. As he grabbed the doorknob to leave the bedroom she said, "oh Junior, zip up your fly before you embarrass yourself," Junior fumbled with his zipper, a brief smile came over his face, as he realized the love of a mother and Mary Kathleen realized a mother's job is never done.

Within moments Junior returned with Naomi at his side. She was wearing a brightly colored dress and shrouded in a white shawl. Mary Kathleen couldn't help but think how different she looked from all the others in their somber attire. "How beautiful you look tonight, Naomi."

"I dozed off in my chair and dreamt that our chief came to me once again dressed in white," she began in a soft voice that was almost an inaudible whisper. "He told me to don colorful clothing for the celebration. This is the outfit I wear for the celebration of light as winter turns to spring, and the light warms Mother Earth in preparation for new life." Mary Kathleen once again fell to the comfort of Naomi's wisdom. She knew from her own Christian belief that Vida was about to enter a new life in a place of light, joy, and peace. She tried to hold on to that comfort, but once again her loss was tugging at her heart.

They administered the three eyedroppers full of herbal medicine, made Vida comfortable, perhaps, more for their own comfort. Once again, the three stood with their arms around each other.

A barren spruce tree stood in the good parlor. The Sexton of the church, Mr. Johnson had decided the family should have a tree. He brought the tree two days earlier; he had placed it in a bucket of coal and water to give it nourishment. Mary Kathleen had already brought the boxes of Christmas decorations from the attic before school had ended for Christmas vacation. On the marble top table behind the sofa was the special decoration, the angel that adorned Mary Kathleen's family tree in her childhood, beside it was the four sterling silver engraved ornaments that portrayed the family with an adult man and woman and a young boy and young girl. The ornaments were inscribed with the full names and dates of birth, John Sr., Mary Kathleen, John Junior, and Vida Rose. The room had an eerie silence and was dimly lit. The only light came from the light hanging over the dining room table casting its light into the silent parlor.

The front door opened, and Dr. Tinker could be seen taking off his hat, scarf, and winter coat. He came to the dining room and greeted everyone looking around the room for Mary Kathleen. Seeing she was not there he ascended the stairs. Within moments Father O'Flaherty entered the front door and immediately went upstairs. Everyone gathered in the dining room and kitchen pondering what to do. They all wanted to return to the bedroom but knew it would be an invasion of privacy and get in the way of doctor and clergy. They waited in idle chat for a few moments and then one or two at a time ascended the stairs and gathered once again.

Dr. Tinker stood rubbing his chin after his examination of the lifeless girl. "Mary Kathleen may I speak with you privately?" he questioned. She immediately led him to the guest bedroom. "Mary Kathleen, I have never seen this before, but Vida Rose is so close to death, but has broken a sweat, which means her fever has broken. We mustn't get our hopes up as she is a very sick girl and quite honestly near death. Her heart is weak, and her respirations aggravated by fluid in her lungs.

But her fever has broken," he said as he grabbed Mary Kathleen's hand holding it in his hand and covering it with the other. Mary Kathleen wanted so badly to hold on to this glimmer of hope.

CHAPTER 7

The new fallen snow had cleansed the earth with a blanket of purity. Father O'Flaherty was chatting with the people gathered at Vida's bedside. The moon bathed the earth in a celestial light. Had the sadness of the situation not been so grievous it would have been a perfect Christmas Eve. Icicles hung at every eave and glistened with the streetlights. It was as if God knew, because of the war, no one could have outside decorations. To be prepared against air raids communities had to be dark. It's as if God decorated the village in accord with Mother Nature. The air was crisp, but not cold. A wonderful New England Christmas Eve.

Father O'Flaherty was becoming anxious as the clock approached the 11th hour. He knew he had

Midnight Mass but felt a genuine duty as a Priest to be with Mary Kathleen and her family in their hour of need. The Mass would be dedicated to Vida Rose. Father had convinced himself he could be a bit late as long as he was there before the Gospel reading so that he could proceed with the Homily. Deacon Mike had been given orders to begin the Mass in Father's absence and to stall things if he could. Father O'Flaherty knew that there would be standing room only at St. Luke's as the whole community knew the beauty of Midnight Mass. They also knew that it was Vida Rose's home parish. The community knew that in his compassion, Father O'Flaherty would allow all people to receive the Sacrament of Holy Communion on Christmas Eve. It just seemed right to gather at the Lord's table in an effort to do something for Vida and her family. Father O'Flaherty was loved by everyone in the community regardless of their faith or denomination. He was a Priest with a true calling to serve humanity. The church could often have rigid rules and regulations that seemed to alienate and segregate people, but Father was flexible and often subconsciously felt that rules were made to be broken, especially if they stood in the way of bringing someone to God. Early in his Priesthood father reckoned with himself that 'faith is of God and religion is of man.

Mary Kathleen sat at Vida's bedside holding her left hand. Mary Kathleen held Vida's tiny hand in the palm of her own hand, rubbing the back of her daughter's hand and with her thumb.

Vida's hand weakly grasped hers and Mary Kathleen felt renewed signs of life in her languished daughter. She dared not say anything as she thought it might be her imagination, simply a reflex action from dehydration. Within herself Mary Kathleen had renewed hope. She closed her eyes and could hear the faint muttering of Hail Mary's and prayers behind her, she offered a prayer of her own in the solitude of her meditation.

"God, on this Holy Night so many years ago you created a family with the birth of your son our Savior Jesus Christ. Please return my family to me, spare the life of my daughter, Vida. I beg you to continue her service to you here on earth rather than heaven, I leave it in your hands and may your will be done. Amen"

Suddenly there was a flapping sound at the window next to where Naomi was sitting. A nearly pure white pigeon had landed on the windowsill outside. Its head bobbed around looking in the window perhaps at its reflection, perhaps out of its own curiosity. Naomi looked at Mary Kathleen. Their eyes became fixed upon each other's, Naomi winked as if acknowledging the bird to be a spiritual message. Mary Kathleen's gaze returned to her daughter's face, and Vida briefly opened her eyes and closed them again immediately.

"My God in heaven, did you see that? She opened her eyes." Mary Kathleen said in a gleeful voice almost shouting. Father O'Flaherty knelt at Mary Kathleen's side placing his hand on the hands of Mary Kathleen and Vida.

"Keep saying her name, she will recognize your voice and come to her mother," Father instructed.

Vida Rose was still in a dreamlike state weakened by the previous days of fever and illness. She continued her winter journey. She looked out the window of the carriage which had returned to the front gate of the castle. The castle was arrayed in beautiful sunlight and carried a warm façade, unlike when she first appeared in front of it so cold. She touched the rose to her lips and the beautiful lady appeared. "My child you have taken a long and difficult journey, but you have made many right decisions, and you have learned from your journey things that will be with you throughout this life and eternity. Carry them well, love and respect the goodness of the spirit that dwells in you."

Vida Rose looked into the lady's eyes. She felt the love and compassion of a soul that offered her refuge during some difficult times. A wise woman that shared her wisdom and her gifts by bringing out Vida Rose's wisdom and gifts.

"It is time for me to go home," Vida acknowledged to the woman but more to herself.

"It is a very right decision," the beautiful lady said as she kissed her on each cheek. Vida opened her eyes to find her mother's lips caressing her cheek with a gentle kiss. In a whisper of a voice Vida Rose said, "Oh Mother, I have taken a beautiful journey and met the most beautiful woman. She was dressed in a long red velvet coat with a white fur cape. I called her the Snow Queen. It's such a long beautiful story."

"I'm sure you did, but you need your rest, thank God you are with us," Mary Kathleen said as she choked back tears.

"What day is it?" Vida inquired.

"It is Christmas Eve and I'm going to be late for Mass," Father O'Flaherty chimed in. "Let us pray, In the name of the Father, and of the Son, and of the Holy Ghost, Oh God, on this evening of remembering the miracles that you brought to earth with the birth of your son Jesus Christ, we give thanks for the return of your servant, our child Vida Rose, nourish her and give her the strength of your spirit to lead the residue of her life on the path you have set before her. We pray this prayer in the name of the Father, and of the Son, and of the Holy Spirit. Amen."

"Now I think it only fitting that we take a moment to sing a song that we all have known from our childhood to honor this evening. He began in his Irish tenor voice, 'Silent Night, Holy Night, All Is Calm, all is bright. Round yon virgin, Mother and child, Holy infant so tender and mild, sleep in heavenly peace, sleep in heavenly peace. Amen"

The room was filled with people gathered at the bedside in awe of what they had witnessed. They had gathered close to hear Vida's faint whispers. Father O'Flaherty was removing his stole, stuffing it into the pocket of his cassock. Suddenly Vida opened her eyes wide and said in a clear strong voice, "father the beautiful lady promised me I would be with you before the day ended and so it is." She stared beyond the people and as they turned to see what she was staring at, there stood her father, John Sr..

"Merry Christmas everyone," as he made his way to his daughter. Mary Kathleen joined the embrace from the other side of the bed, and John Junior jumped on his father's back.

Left standing in the opening where the people had parted to let John closer to the bed, stood a man on crutches. He had a cast on his leg up to his knee. "Saints preserve us, you old fool," Naomi said as she kissed her husband on the cheek and laid the side of her face over his heart.

The choir from St. Luke's had gathered outside along with many of the parishioners knowing that

Father O'Flaherty was late. Once again, it seemed there was a celestial chorus singing 'Silent Night,' along with a host of Angels and Archangels and all the company of the heavens.

It truly was a Merry Christmas!

The End

ABOUT THE AUTHOR

Phil Jordan grew up in a small community in Upstate New York. He holds an Associate of Arts Degree in Humanities and Social Science, a Bachelor's Degree in Secondary Education in Spanish, and a Master's Degree in Education with an emphasis in Counseling. He is a graduate of New York State Municipal Police Academy having been a sworn deputy with the Tioga County Sheriff's Department affiliating with agencies throughout the country. He is also a graduate of Simmons School of Mortuary Science in Syracuse NY and has been a Licensed Funeral Director for the past 35 years.

Phil has been an ordained Non-Denominational Minister for the past 35 years, serving two parishes, The Caroline Center Church in Brooktondale, NY, and St. Luke's Chapel in Van Etten, NY.

He self-published his biography, *I Knew This Day Would Come,* and a children's book and workbook on grief, *Mrs. Quigley Died One Day.*

He is a Nationally and Internationally known Psychic for the past 60 years, whose success in police work has facilitated 20 episodes on Court TV, Psychic Detective, ABC and YouTube. He hosted weekly radio shows in his work for five years in the Binghamton and Elmira NY areas.

He has garnered wisdom from all his professions, as well as life, to create the story, *A Winter's Journey*. A story that spontaneously came to him while driving one sunny day. A story that came from the depths of his psyche and psychic self to be shared as a spiritual gift for others.

Made in United States
North Haven, CT
20 January 2026